THE MUMMY CODE

Level 4H

Written by Melanie Hamm
Illustrated by Roger Simo

What is synthetic phonics?

Synthetic phonics teaches children to recognise the sounds of letters and to blend (synthesise) them together to make whole words.

Understanding sound/letter relationships gives children the confidence and ability to read unfamiliar words, without having to rely on memory or guesswork; this helps them to progress towards independent reading.

Did you know? Spoken English uses more than 40 speech sounds. Each sound is called a *phoneme*. Some phonemes relate to a single letter (d-o-g) and others to combinations of letters (sh-ar-p). When a phoneme is written down it is called a *grapheme*. Teaching these sounds, matching them to their written form and sounding out words for reading is the basis of synthetic phonics.

Consultant

I love reading phonics has been created in consultation with language expert Abigail Steel. She has a background in teaching and teacher training and is a respected expert in the field of synthetic phonics. Abigail Steel is a regular contributor to educational publications. Her international education consultancy supports parents and teachers in the promotion of literacy skills.

Reading tips

This book focuses on the oa sound, made with the letter formation o-e, as in home.

Tricky words in this book

Any words in bold may have unusual spellings or are new and have not yet been introduced.

> Tricky words in this book:
>
> ## mystery golden strange knew there symbols saw would stretched treasure half awesome voice

Extra ways to have fun with this book

After the reader has read the story, ask them questions about what they have just read:

What did Ambrose discover in the tunnel?

What was your favourite part of the story?

This must be a secret code... but what does it mean?

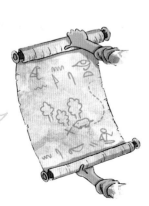

A pronunciation guide

This grid contains the sounds used in the stories in levels 4, 5 and 6 and a guide on how to say them. /a/ represents the sounds made, rather than the letters in a word.

/ai/ as in game	/ai/ as in play/they	/ee/ as in leaf/these	/ee/ as in he
/igh/ as in kite/light	/igh/ as in find/sky	/oa/ as in home	/oa/ as in snow
/oa/ as in cold	/y+oo/ as in cube/music/new	long /oo/ as in flute/crew/blue	/oi/ as in boy
/er/ as in bird/hurt	/or/ as in snore/oar/door	/or/ as in dawn/sauce/walk	/e/ as in head
/e/ as in said/any	/ou/ as in cow	/u/ as in touch	/air/ as in hare/bear/there
/eer/ as in deer/here/cashier	/t/ as in tripped/skipped	/d/ as in rained	/j/ as in gent/gin/gym
/j/ as in barge/hedge	/s/ as in cent/circus/cyst	/s/ as in prince	/s/ as in house
/ch/ as in itch/catch	/w/ as in white	/h/ as in who	/r/ as in write/rhino

Sounds this story focuses on
are highlighted in the grid.

/**f**/ as in phone	/**f**/ as in rough	/**ul**/ as in pencil/ hospital	/**z**/ as in fries/ cheese/breeze
/**n**/ as in knot/ gnome/engine	/**m**/ as in welcome /thumb/column	/**g**/ as in guitar/ghost	/**zh**/ as in vision/beige
/**k**/ as in chord	/**k**/ as in plaque/ bouquet	/**nk**/ as in uncle	/**ks**/ as in box/books/ ducks/cakes
/**a**/ and /**o**/ as in hat/what	/**e**/ and /**ee**/ as in bed/he	/**i**/ and /**igh**/ as in fin/find	/**o**/ and /**oa**/ as in hot/cold
/**u**/ and short /**oo**/ as in but/put	/**ee**/, /**e**/ and /**ai**/ as in eat/ bread/break	/**igh**/, /**ee**/ and /**e**/ as in tie/field/friend	/**ou**/ and /**oa**/ as in cow/blow
/**ou**/, /**oa**/ and /**oo**/ as in out/ shoulder/could	/**i**/ and /**ai**/ as in money/they	/**c**/ and /**s**/ as in cat/cent	/**y**/, /**igh**/ and /**i**/ as in yes/sky/myth
/**g**/ and /**j**/ as in got/giant	/**ch**/, /**c**/ and /**sh**/ as in chin/ school/chef	/**er**/, /**air**/ and /**eer**/ as in earth/bear/ears	/**u**/, /**ou**/ and /**oa**/ as in plough/dough

Be careful not to add an 'uh' sound to 's', 't', 'p',
'c', 'h', 'r', 'm', 'd', 'g', 'l', 'f' and 'b'. For example,
say 'fff' not 'fuh' and 'sss' not 'suh'.

Ambrose Jones had a nose
for **mystery**. So when he dug
up a **golden** box with a

strange note inside, he **knew** he must decode it.

"**There** is a mole. Well, a mole digs. And those trees are a grove... I need to dig in a grove!" Ambrose supposed.

He rode until he found a grove –
a brilliant stroke of luck!

Ambrose dug a hole until he
found a tunnel. But the tunnel

sloped both ways. Ambrose chose
left and hoped he was right!

On the stone wall there were
more **symbols**: a robe and
a throne.

"Hmm," Ambrose pondered.
"Whose home is this?"

"Mine!" came a muffled tone.
Ambrose froze.

He was not alone!

In an alcove he **saw** a casket.
Ambrose crept close.

The **voice** spoke: "You woke me!
Now let me out!"

Ambrose was choked with fear.
But he broke the seal and lifted
the lid.

Would he see bones?
No!
A mummy rose from the casket!

The mummy **stretched** and
strode around. "I have dozed
too long! My bones are stiff!"
the mummy joked.

"Now, Ambrose Jones, can you crack this one last code?" The mummy pointed to a coin and a crown.

"A **treasure** trove!" cried
Ambrose Jones.
"Come and look!" the mummy
proposed.

"Long ago I was king of **half** the globe!"

Ambrose Jones had a nose for mystery. "**Awesome**!" he said.

OVER 48 TITLES IN SIX LEVELS
Abigail Steel recommends...

Other titles to enjoy from Level 4

I love reading phonics — **The Circus Mice**
978-1-84898-582-7

I love reading phonics — **Monster's Night**
978-1-84898-583-4

I love reading phonics — **Jemima The Spy**
978-1-84898-584-1

Some titles from Level 5

I love reading phonics — **The Gigantic Bear**
978-1-84898-586-5

I love reading phonics — **Celebrity Celia**
978-1-84898-587-2

I love reading phonics — **The Cemetery Dance**
978-1-84898-588-9

Some titles from Level 6

I love reading phonics — **Hugh is New**
978-1-84898-590-2

I love reading phonics — **Clumsy Eagle**
978-1-84898-591-9

I love reading phonics — **Bad Zombie Movie**
978-1-84898-592-6

An Hachette UK Company
www.hachette.co.uk

Copyright © Octopus Publishing Group Ltd 2012
First published in Great Britain in 2012 by TickTock, an imprint of Octopus Publishing Group Ltd,
Endeavour House, 189 Shaftesbury Avenue, London WC2H 8JY.
www.octopusbooks.co.uk

ISBN 978 1 84898 585 8

Printed and bound in China
10 9 8 7 6 5 4 3 2 1